Doogie and the Rollers

Sharif Islam

First published 2014
Published by GB Publishing.org

A catalogue record of the printed book is available from
the British Library

Cover Design © Mary Pargeter Design

CBP.
GB Publishing.org
www.gbpublishing.org

For
Poo lovers everywhere who want to enjoy
an adventure and a giggle

Acknowledgement

Grateful thanks to the following for their unrelenting support, encouragement and friendship:

Lisa Chandler, Jena Al-Bazi, Bizhan Shokouhi, Zuzana Repkova, Natalia Kyselova, Eugene Lowenkopf, Martin Soska, Gareth Jones, Pam and Steve Soudry, Christopher Ritchie, Mohit Ramchandani, and my dear mum, Azizun.

Contents

ONE

"Get your hands off my poo!"

Doogie was angry and fed up. Almost every time he or one of the other Rollers managed to carefully roll their collected dung into a perfectly formed ball, the Dwellers would come along and try to steal it. On this occasion, however, it was just one of General Proctor's soldiers, Lieutenant Choker. For a dung beetle, Choker was unusually tall and muscular with angular features and never without his belt and baton. To most of the other dung beetles he was someone to be feared. General Proctor, the leader of the Dwellers, took great pride in this fact, never hesitating to send his lieutenant on these raids.

"I don't think you understand," said Lieutenant Choker, pushing his face against Doogie's. The sun beating down onto the arid African plains cast a menacing shadow from Choker's pronounced brow, such that his fearsome eyes pierced through large round pools of black. "This is not a negotiation. I'm taking that fresh, sticky ball of poo and there's nothing you pathetic little Rollers can do about it."

"You can't have it, Choker. Rolled dung belongs to the Rollers. You're a Dweller, so go and *dwell* somewhere. Find your own pile of poo to stick your big fat head into!"

"We Dwellers take our dung wherever we find it," snapped Choker. "And unless you want me to take out my baton, I suggest you *back off! Now!*"

Doogie was very stubborn for a dung beetle, and not one to back down easily. He had less fear than his fellow Rollers and wanted to stand up to the Dwellers, whom he regarded as nothing more than thugs. But as heavily as his pride weighed upon his toughened heart, he knew Choker's baton could do some damage, and that Choker wouldn't hesitate to use it. Many of his friends had been beaten by it, and in the end self-preservation was more important than bravado. But he thought he might as well stay up in Choker's face for just a few seconds more.

Unfortunately for Doogie's pride, Choker's huge angular face had blocked his view of the sprawling savannah and he failed to notice that General Proctor's daughter Hoya had silently crept up behind them.

As Doogie started to back down, his hurt pride suddenly turned to humiliation in front of this beautiful dung beetle. He had had an obvious crush on her ever since he had morphed from a tiny larva into a beetle himself.

Hoya was a vision of perfection to Doogie; slender and pretty, with big, inviting eyes and an elegance that was most unlike her species. An almost luminescent green, she was one of the few of her kind that actually didn't smell of poo. It was remarkable, Doogie always thought, that she could be the daughter of the tyrannical General. And even more so that a Dweller could be so beautiful and gentle. How could someone like that belong to a bunch of thieving bandits?

As Choker pushed him aside and grabbed the ball of dung, the dejected Doogie raised an embarrassed eyebrow to catch Hoya's expression, half expecting her to look disappointed in him. Instead he found her staring at him sympathetically, enough that he raised his other eyebrow until both of his surprised eyes met hers. Choker walked away, ball of dung in tow, and beckoned at Hoya to follow him with a grunt.

But Hoya clasped her hands together and started to speak, making Doogie blush and tremble, and blush even more as he tried to hide it.

"Hi Doogie. Listen…I just wanted to say…that I'm really…"

"Hoya!" Choker called. "We have what we came for. We're leaving."

Hoya looked into Doogie's eyes for an extra moment, as if sensing his loss and embarrassment.

3

"Now!" insisted Choker.

Hoya gently raised and bent her fingers at Doogie to signal the slightest of waves, then turned and left.

~~~

Not a good day. It had taken all afternoon to roll that dung into a ball, only to have it taken away by a brutish thug. And worse still, in front of the girl he was crazy about. Sweltering in his blue tinted shield, Doogie sat in the hot sand and pondered his misfortune. The ground sprawled out for miles, baked and charred under a cloudless sky with a solitary sun. He would return to his clan of Rollers empty-handed and humiliated, despite having urged them for so long to stand up to the Dwellers. He could hardly contemplate having to find another big pile of poo in amongst the herds of wildebeest, elephants and zebras.

He stared so low into the ground he almost failed to notice the darkness washing over him. But it wasn't night-time already. It was a massive shadow. And it belonged to the very kind elephant that had earlier produced the enormous pile of poo for Doogie to harvest.

A giant trunk gently nudged Doogie, as if testing him for signs of life. Then it sniffed at his scent, inhaling the vapours of poo and recognising it as its own. There was nothing of

4

interest here other than a downhearted dung beetle so the elephant casually strolled on, once again revealing the daylight in its wake. But as it did so it turned back to look at Doogie, and a torrent of slimy poo gushed from its behind, splashing onto the ground with such a thud that Doogie was knocked onto his feet.

Although in no mood to roll more clumps of its splatter into neat balls, he thanked the elephant with a salute and shuffled his way to the huge steaming pile it had kindly left behind. He might as well bring something back to the colony.

But something else grabbed Doogie's attention. A flickering shadow began swirling around on the ground, circling his position and becoming larger and larger. Heat from the elephant's poo blurred the savannah into a haze and the aroma was so strong it overwhelmed Doogie's antennae. By the time he had realised what was overhead and looked up, he was already in the unshakeable grip of the eagle's talons.

TWO

He had never felt a breeze like this, rushing against him and delivering smells from all over the plains. The elephant and zebra poo was very familiar, but the stench of lions and hyena were in the air too. Howler monkeys have a subtle scent to their poo, and Doogie could also hear their vocal racket from the distance. It was a blistering hurricane of aromas brushing past his antennae, and too much for one little dung beetle to even think about sorting through.

The landscape emerged from a blur to reveal a strangely shimmering valley, reflecting the sun across it as speckles of light. It was far into the distance, but Doogie could just make out the herds of beasts gathered in the valley. Some were feeding on lush green grass and others were gleefully unloading their bowels onto it. Mountains of poo seemed to line the sides of the valley, which appeared to end at a large pyramidal structure. It was golden brown and blindingly bright, but Doogie couldn't focus properly. The raging gusts of air beneath him were tickling his legs and…

Wait…beneath him?! Doogie suddenly realised that he was high up in the skies above the savannah he called home, strangled inside the gigantic talons of an eagle. The eagle was absolutely enormous, with a menacing snarl in its bright yellow

6

beak and the blackest of eyes that seared their glare through the world in front of them. Its wings blocked out the sky as it glided on currents, and its talons were as hard as rock, probably barely aware of the tiny, petrified dung beetle in their grip.

Doogie had momentarily blacked out after being taken and, now awake, his wonderment quickly cascaded into complete panic. He knew at any moment the eagle could crush his delicate shield and feed off the remains.

But as much as fear took hold with the eagle's grip, Doogie also knew he was not destined to end this way. He still had so much to do, so much poo to enjoy. And Hoya, his first and only love, would never know how he felt. She would never even know what had happened to him; that he was brutally snatched from her by a monstrous eagle. He just couldn't allow that to happen. As the dry, hot air washed over him, his brain began to spin ideas on how to escape.

The eagle swooped low over the flat savannah, as if racing with the marauding herd of wildebeest below. There were thousands of them, drumming and grunting as they raced ahead, struggling not to trip over each other while desperate to evade the eagle's threat. The eagle circled over them before soaring back into the sky. It was all Doogie could do not to throw up. The speed of the eagle was both exhilarating and terrifying for him, and for a moment he relished having a fantastic story to tell his friends. Assuming he survived.

Another dive through a tree and the branches rattled past, shedding their leaves into the air. One of the leaves smacked Doogie in the face, covering him almost whole like a big green blanket. He could hardly breathe. The leaf started to irritate his face and he knew straight away it was a citrus leaf. As the eagle gained speed, the oncoming wind pressed the leafy blanket harder against Doogie's face until he could feel an intense burning sensation.

He knew he had only moments left, suffocating under a poisonous leaf and paralysed in the vice of the eagle's talons. He had little choice. All his life he had only tasted a varied menu of creamy poo from the biggest beasts on the land. Now, if he was to survive, he knew he had to fight through the horrible taste of this leaf and chew it out of his way.

He started munching, and the air flooded back at him through the bites. It tasted revolting and began burning his mouth but at least he wasn't suffocating. Each begrudging chew was worse than the last, until Doogie could stand it no longer. The burning sensation had become too painful. He spat it all out and the wind pinned the flecks of green, chewed up leaf against the eagle's legs.

The eagle began screeching loudly and wildly, its wings flapping violently. Doogie's ears were hurting from the noise, but worse than that, the eagle started spiralling downwards, screaming in pain. And then Doogie saw it. The spat-out leafy flecks were burning the eagle's legs, making red blotches appear all over them.

As dizzy as Doogie was becoming while hurtling through the air, he was still conscious enough to notice that the talons were loosening their grip. Here was his chance! Doogie wriggled violently with all his might, spitting more of the chewed leaf onto the talons. He dared not look below as the savannah became closer on its way up to meet him, but he continued wriggling and struggling.

And suddenly, the talons opened up. Air rushed in. Doogie was free.

Free and falling.

~~~

His landing was softer than he imagined; not the hard, crashing halt he was expecting. He was on his back looking up, the eagle soaring away into a tiny, screeching speck in the sky. He rolled onto his legs, looked ahead, and saw a mattress of black and white stripes laid out before him. He had landed on a zebra.

Being so much bigger, the zebra had hardly noticed a small and bewildered dung beetle landing on its back. It was too engrossed in chewing through mouthfuls of grass to even feel Doogie crawl across its back towards its hind legs. But the tickle of a beetle abseiling down its tail was too much for the zebra. As Doogie finally landed on firm ground, the umbrella of zebra tail above him angled upwards and a ferocious shower of thick, warm poo utterly drenched him.

And it was just heavenly.

THREE

"You'll never guess what happened to me."

After hours of walking and distilling various faecal aromas from around the savannah, Doogie had finally arrived back at the Rollers' colony. He found his best friends, Clinker and Brownie, waiting for him in his own dung hut.

"It smells like you took a shower in zebra poo," said Clinker, a gluttonous, plump and clumsy dung beetle, always thinking with his stomach. His considerable bulk was lazily spread over the floor of Doogie's dung hut, and his chubby face displayed no apparent concern that his best friend had not been seen or heard from for several hours.

"Yes I did, but before that," said Doogie.

"Is it fresh?" asked Clinker.

"Is what fresh?" Doogie was impatient to get his story out.

"The zebra poo," Clinker replied, hungrily eyeing the smears of dung still attached to Doogie's shield.

"No, it's a few hours old."

"You know, their stripe patterns are unique," announced Brownie as he inhaled deeply.

"What?!" huffed Doogie.

"Zebras. They each have unique stripe patterns." Brownie couldn't resist any opportunity to show off his encyclopaedic

11

knowledge. His nerdish and sinewy build seemed to perfectly fit his professorial manner, and he was utterly content to lean against the wall inside the dung hut and deliver factual commentary on anything that was being said. "I detect a hint of citrus too. Are we spicing up our meals these days?"

"I don't care how old it is or where it came from, or whether it has stripes or spots," said Clinker. "I'm hungry."

"Look!" started an exasperated Doogie. "Can we just forget about the zebra poo for one moment? I have to tell you what happened to me."

And so Doogie laid out the entire episode, from Choker's theft of his dung to being kidnapped by the eagle, enacting the events and mimicking both by waving his arms about wildly. He told of how he landed on the zebra's back and spent the next few hours searching for the Rollers, with only luck preventing him from being squashed by traffic jams of mighty beasts along the way.

"You could have flown back here. We do have wings, after all," said Clinker.

"Yes," added Brownie, "But we're used to flying only short distances. We don't have the energy for much else. There's a reason we have six limbs, you know."

"My wings aren't in great shape anyway," said Doogie. "I haven't used them in so long I forgot I have them."

"Was Hoya there?" asked Brownie. Clinker frowned at him, knowing it was a sensitive subject for Doogie. But Brownie innocently shrugged his shoulders and stared at Doogie, who bowed his head low in shame at the very mention of Hoya.

"Yes," he said, sheepishly.

"You need to let that go, Doogs," said Brownie. "She's a Dweller. You can't possibly get near her. You'll die trying."

"I think..." began Doogie, clearly embarrassed by the topic, "I think…she likes me."

"Be that as it may," said Clinker, "she's the General's daughter. He'd quite happily baste you in elephant poo and eat you for lunch before letting you anywhere near her. Face it. There's just no way. Rollers and Dwellers will never mix."

But this only fermented Doogie's embarrassment into anger, and he hopped onto his hind legs and clenched his front fists.

"We have to stand up to those thugs! How can we just let them keep stealing our poo? I mean, there's an entire world of poo out there. The beasts are dropping it all over the place all the time. Why do we let them take ours?"

"It's always been this way," said Brownie. "So it was, and so it shall be. It's just the way things are."

"Well, it's wrong!" Doogie exclaimed. "Just wrong."

13

"Who are we to change it?" asked Clinker, sprawling his fat legs even more and yawning. "I mean, it's not like we're living in Dungalore."

"Dungalore's a myth, anyway," said Brownie.

"What in the name of faeces is Dungalore?" asked Doogie.

"Seriously?" said Clinker. "You've never heard of Dungalore? Didn't your parents tell you the tale when you were younger?"

"My parents were killed by an eagle when I was younger. So, what's Dungalore?"

"Well…" began Clinker, and he recounted the entire tale to Doogie of a magical valley of poo, where dung beetles were once revered and entirely at peace with the beasts supplying them with their endless waste to recycle. The dung was abundant and sweet and there were no Rollers or Dwellers, just dung beetles living together in harmony. Even the eagles kept their distance.

"They used to call us scarabs," said Brownie. "We were worshipped at one point. The human beasts even made little statues and ornaments of us."

"Yeah, they probably liked having us around to clean up their poo," suggested Clinker.

"No, Clinks. It wasn't that at all. I think our parents were trying to tell us there was a time when we were so important

14

that even the most dominant of beasts felt they needed us. We are pretty important to the world, after all. Who else cleans up and recycles all that waste? Without us the entire world would just be a ginormous pile of poo."

"Well, that sounds pretty awesome to me." Clinker's gaze wandered off as he tried to imagine it.

"Where was this place?" asked Doogie, clearly mesmerised by the very idea of it.

"I'm not really sure," answered Brownie. "But it's supposed to be under the Constellation Big Dumper, which kind of looks like the big plough thingy that the human beasts use to tear up the ground. The story goes that the humans built some kind of monuments to us. A huge pyramid stood at the end of the valley. All the beasts would come and poo all over the…"

"Wait," interrupted Doogie. "Did you say pyramid?"

"Yeah. Why?"

"I think I've seen this place."

"Er…sorry to shatter your hopes, buddy," said Clinker, "but it's just a myth. It doesn't actually exist."

"Well, how do you know that it never existed? Look, when I was flying around up there with the eagle…"

"You mean when the eagle grabbed you off the ground and carried you away in his claws, presumably to eat you?" Despite the hint of sarcasm, Brownie was a stickler for details.

"Yeah, okay, whatever," Doogie said impatiently. "But when I was up there, I know I saw a place like the one you're describing. I know there was some kind of pyramid there. At the end of a valley."

Clinker and Brownie looked at each other with obvious disbelief on their faces.

"Look," said Doogie. "I know it sounds crazy, and you only just told me about this place. But I know I'm right. I've seen it from the sky. How many times have you guys seen the world from the sky?"

"Er...*never*, I hope," said Clinker. "I prefer to walk on the ground."

"This citrus leaf that you ate," inquired Brownie. "I wonder if it has any effects on the mind? Like believing in things that don't exist?"

"Very funny," said Doogie. "Look, I think if..."

Doogie's train of thought was interrupted by a sensation at his feet. He could feel a low but increasing vibration. Brownie could feel it too.

"What is that?" asked Brownie.

"What's what?" asked Clinker.

"That vibration. Can't you feel it?"

"I thought that was my stomach telling me I'm hungry."

16

"Your stomach is always hungry. It's doesn't always sound like that."

"Quiet, you guys." Doogie pressed his ear against the wall. "It's getting louder." His antennae perked up. "And…wait – can you smell that?"

"Did you just fart?" asked Clinker.

"Clinks, be serious for a second, would you?" Brownie frowned.

"It sounds like a lot of feet marching towards us," said Doogie. "And it smells like…"

"Like what?" asked Brownie.

Doogie turned and looked anxiously at his friends, the hairs on his arms and legs standing up.

"I think we need to go outside."

FOUR

Doogie and his friends stood outside the dung hut in the darkening blue dusk. Other Rollers had stepped outside their huts too, all gripped with trepidation. Facing them were a small army of Dwellers carrying small batons shaped from tiny twigs, a look of menace on their faces.

"What is this?" demanded Doogie, defiance in his tone. "What are you doing here?"

A gap opened in the middle of the Dwellers, as half shuffled one way and half the other, synchronised with military precision. The parting quickly reached the centre of the group to reveal two dung beetles with all feet on the ground and harnesses around their bodies. Reins led back from them to a large black chariot constructed from hardened black dung and with a rolled ball of dung for a wheel underneath. And standing in the chariot, high above the other Dwellers, was the imposing frame of General Proctor.

"This…" began the General in his booming, gravelly voice, "…is a collection. We are collecting your dung."

The General didn't flinch in his statement. His huge chest arched forward with arms folded behind his back and his round, dimpled chin angled upwards. Attached to his baldric were dozens of sharpened twigs. His waist belt held a baton on

18

each side. Staring into the sky above, his steely eyes were barely visible. Only the horn above his mouth and antennae on each side of his head reached up from under the black beret pulled low over his brow. His chariot was a shiny black throne, simple in its design but intimidating in its height. It sat just forward of the ball of black dung underneath it, which in turn had black twigs on either side to anchor the harnesses from the beetles in front.

"You're not having our dung, General," said Doogie. Clinker and Brownie looked at him in amazement that he would answer back.

"Really?" said General Proctor. At that moment, the broad outline of Lieutenant Choker emerged from the shadows behind the chariot, his evil grin and beady eyes piercing through the darkness ahead of the rest of his face.

Doogie stood his ground and didn't move. Clinker and Brownie were terrified and it was all they could do to stop emptying their own bowels. Choker approached them all, once again pressing his massive face against Doogie's.

"Don't you remember what happened the last time we met?" Choker asked. "As I recall, you were a lot more…co-operative."

Doogie said nothing, in part because of the considerable lump of fear that had been growing in his throat. He knew that all eyes were watching him, and his stubbornness compelled him to defy Choker for as long as he could get away with. But as threatening as Choker was, he was nothing compared to the mighty General Proctor, who could have his army destroy the entire Roller compound with a click of his fingers.

Choker leaned back from Doogie with a creeping sneer and clasped his hand around his baton. "Well, it looks like I am going to have the pleasure of using this after all."

Gasps from the other Rollers were audible above the tension, but still Doogie stood firm. So did Clinker and Brownie, but only because they were paralysed with fear and didn't know what else to do.

"But wait," continued Choker. "If we're going to have some entertainment, then we might as well have an audience." He turned back towards the army of waiting Dwellers and with a wave of his hand signalled for some of them to move aside. And as they shuffled apart, the radiant figure of Hoya appeared, her lustrous green shield almost glowing in the dusky blue evening light. She slowly raised her bowed head to look at Doogie, a pained expression upon her face. Doogie realised instantly that she didn't want to be there, and he resented Choker's sadistic ploy even more.

General Proctor, protective of his only daughter, drew his gaze across from Hoya to Choker. "Lieutenant. Make it quick."

"With pleasure." Choker grinned. And as he held aloft his baton, the Dweller army began to charge in every direction, running through and over the Rollers' dung huts and their inhabitants.

Doogie tucked his head down against his chest as Choker's baton crashed down onto the shield on his back, knocking him flat against the ground. Clinker and Brownie ran instantly in opposite directions, not wanting to share the same fate. Choker proceeded to tear down the dung huts, smashing them with his baton, and directing the soldiers to carry away the pieces.

The other Rollers ran for cover, hiding in the nearby shrubs, from where they could only watch the unfolding raid and its destruction of their homes. Dung was flying everywhere, and neatly rolled balls became dismantled piles. The Dwellers were relentless, tearing apart every bit of dung they could find and scaring away the Rollers they found with them. General Proctor remained in his chariot, casually surveying the operation.

Doogie struggled to get to his feet, Choker's baton having knocked the air out of him. A hand reached forward to help him, which Doogie instinctively took hold of to prop himself back onto his feet. As he stood up straight, he saw whom the hand belonged to. It was Hoya. She looked at him expectantly, as if waiting for his reaction, and smiled. Doogie was

21

somewhat speechless, but wanted desperately to say thank you. But before he could force the words out, Hoya noticed her father's head rotating to look in their direction.

Without time to explain, and with the General's gaze almost upon them, Hoya pushed Doogie back onto the ground just in time for the General to see what appeared to be his daughter hitting a petulant Roller. A wry and subtle smile formed along the General's mouth.

"Hoya," he boomed. "We're done here."

At first bewildered, Doogie turned around to see the General watching and Hoya's clever deception suddenly dawned on him. He smiled at her and, wanting to maintain the ruse, began holding his chest as if in pain. Hoya realised that Doogie had understood her ploy and kicked him a few times.

"Ow!" he yelped, glaring at Hoya as if to tell her she might be over-playing the part.

But Hoya, whose face couldn't be seen by her father behind her, smiled and winked at Doogie, before running off.

As the Dweller army began to coalesce back towards the General's chariot, Doogie sat on the ground, momentarily oblivious of the wanton destruction that had by now laid the Rollers' compound to waste. His heart was racing and his elated thoughts were spinning around in his head too fast for him to collect. Hoya had protected him, even collaborated with him, despite the watchful eye of her father. To Doogie, that was confirmation that she definitely liked him.

As he sat pondering this wonderful thought, he failed to notice that Choker had been standing behind him in the ruins of his dung hut. The snarly Lieutenant stepped out of the scraps of what remained and casually walked past Doogie's battered body, looking down at him with utter contempt as he slinked away into the night.

Doogie got back onto his feet and looked around him. The rest of his Roller colony slowly emerged from their hiding places to find their homes destroyed and their dung gone. Scraps of dung lay strewn all over the ground in a chaotic mess. Nothing was left intact. Many of the Rollers were crying, uncertain about what to do with the remains of their homes. Clinker and Brownie were amongst them, visibly upset and demoralised, holding in their hands bits of poo that had belonged to their walls.

That was it. That was the last straw, the very last droplet of poo that Doogie was willing to give up. He was beyond anger now.

And he was going do something about it.

FIVE

"I'm going to find Dungalore."

Doogie's announcement to Clinker and Brownie was not met with the enthusiasm he was hoping for. Many of the other Rollers were preoccupied with salvaging the dung that remained after the Dwellers' raid so that they could build new homes in the morning. They used what ration of light the crescent Moon gave them to gather whatever they could find. They had little time or interest in the fantasy of a long lost valley of poo. Many took comfort in the fact that they had no larvae to lose this time of year.

"Look, Doogs," said Clinker, "I realise you're upset and angry. But dreaming of a place that doesn't exist isn't going to brighten your day or make the Dwellers stay away. We need to go out there and get some fresh dung to rebuild."

"So that they can steal it again?!" cried Doogie. "No! They're not doing that. Look at this place. We've got nothing left here. I'm so sick of this happening all the time."

"We're fed up too," said Brownie. "But we can't fight them. They're aggressive by nature. We're not."

"I'm not suggesting we fight them," said Doogie. "Although I wouldn't mind taking Choker's baton and shoving it up his…"

"Er...yes, we get that," finished Clinker.

"What if we can go to this place where we can never be harmed? Where we'll always have as much poo as we want. Where the Dwellers will never find us. Where eagles will never attack us. Who *wouldn't* want that?"

As Clinker and Brownie listened sympathetically to Doogie, all three of them had failed to notice that the other Rollers had overheard the talk of Dungalore. They had stopped clearing up and started listening to the discussion. They all knew the story of Dungalore, but had never heard anyone speak of going there.

Brownie rested his hands around the middle of his skinny frame. "You're expecting us to leave this place we call home and go looking for a place that our parents told us about in a bedtime story?"

"I *know* it's out there," said Doogie. "You may not believe me. But I know I've seen it. And I *know* I can find it."

"How?" asked Clinker, who was trying very discretely to empty handfuls of poo into his chubby mouth as he spoke.

"We'll follow the wildebeest," answered Doogie. "I think they were headed there. And at night, we just need to look for the Constellation Big Dumper. The valley will be under it. Maybe miles and miles away, but it'll be under the Big Dumper."

Clinker and Brownie looked at each other as if each was hoping the other would have something profound to say. But nothing came. Doogie turned away and looked up at the carpet of stars in the night sky above him. "If I have to," he said more solemnly, "I'll find it alone." And with that thought, he lay down to rest for the night.

~~~

The next morning arrived quickly and Doogie presented himself to the rest of the waking Roller colony. Clinker was still chewing on morsels of what used to be his roof while Brownie was helping another Roller roll the last gathered scrap of dung into a ball.

"Hey," called Doogie.

Clinker suddenly stopped chewing and gulped down his last mouthful. Brownie stopped rolling, and he and the other Rollers approached Doogie.

"So, I'll be going," Doogie continued, struggling to look at his friends. "Like, right now. I just wanted to say goodbye."

"So, you've made up your mind?" asked Clinker.

"Yeah. I'm going. I'll...I'll see ya. Maybe." Head bowed, he slowly turned to walk away. He could feel everyone's eyes watching him as made his way out into the savannah. Even with his first few steps he felt the loneliness take hold, the sorrow of leaving his friends behind creeping in. He looked out ahead of him, the land awash with heat and dry air. The epic journey he now faced began to dawn on him.

But as he walked he noticed that each shuffling step he took somehow felt heavier. The ground began to slowly vibrate in tandem with his footsteps, as if many more feet were marching together with his own. Doogie stopped and his heart sank away in fear of another Dweller attack.

"The thing is…" suddenly came Brownie's voice from behind him. Doogie immediately turned around to find every Roller standing together facing him, Clinker and Brownie at the front, and the rolled ball of dung alongside them. "We're coming with you." Brownie walked up to the surprised Doogie, who was just then becoming overwhelmed with relief.

"You were right," continued Brownie. "We all talked about it last night while you were sleeping. We have nothing left here. We have nothing to lose anymore and even if we don't find this place, at least we'll be someplace else where the Dwellers won't find us. We stick together, right?"

Doogie clenched his jaw and fought back the tear welling in his grateful eyes. Clinker came and put his chubby hand on Doogie's shoulder. "And besides," he said. "You didn't think I'd let you eat all that poo by yourself, did you?"

Doogie and the Rollers all burst out laughing. And together, they trailed out towards their new adventure.

SIX

The Dweller colony was humming with the bustle of beetles scuffling over their stolen loot of dung. They each tried to grab messy handfuls and add it to their growing mound, but every time loose scraps would fall from their hands onto the ground. Over time the scraps had become trampled on so much that they formed a hardened carpet. The tall mound housed hastily dug rooms with open entrances, and plenty of little gaps in the walls. The Dwellers were in quite a frenzy over the new dung and happily scurried all over each other with their scraps, leaving trails all around their mound.

General Proctor surveyed the scene from within his own regal dung hut at the edge of the colony. His hut was a large, oval but very dark atrium, with several small round windows carefully cut out at eye level around its circumference. They seemed to be suited more for looking out than for allowing light in. As a blade of light seared in through one such window and bathed the General, Hoya entered the hut and tentatively approached her father. His profile was an outline of a brilliant, bright white glow, tracing around the formidable features of his huge frame.

"Dad?" Hoya delicately brushed her fingers against her father's arm.

"Hoya!" The General almost sang her name with pride. He was always happy to see her. As brutal as he could be, he had an undeniable soft spot for his only daughter. "What can I do for you, my dear?"

"I was thinking," said Hoya, taking comfort from her father's hand around her shoulder. "Why do we keep stealing all our dung from the Rollers? It just seems…well…it seems really unfair to them. I mean, don't they have to work hard for their dung? To collect it and roll it?"

The General smiled reassuringly at his daughter. "My dear child, this is how it has always been. The Rollers are weak. They are workers. We are soldiers. We are made to take dung when we want it."

"But it just seems so cruel," said Hoya, looking through the window at all the activity outside.

"Cruelty doesn't come into it," said the General in his low, gruff voice, tugging Hoya closer to him to comfort her. "It's just the way things are done."

General Proctor then left his daughter at the window and walked to the doorway of the dung hut, where he was met by the silhouette of Lieutenant Choker.

"Choker, see to it that the beetles have their dung rations and ready them for the next raid."

30

"Yes, General," hissed Choker, who had noticed Hoya at the window and approached her as the General left. He stood beside her and pretended to look outside the window with her, but he was actually spying her through the corners of his eyes.

"I couldn't help overhearing your discussion with the General," he said. "You wouldn't be feeling sympathy for those pathetic little Rollers, now, would you?"

"Of course not," Hoya replied firmly, not wanting to look up at the Lieutenant in case he saw her blushing from her lie.

"Good. I would hate to think you had developed a soft spot for your friend."

"What friend?"

"The little weakling you smiled and winked at. Or was I mistaken?"

"I have no idea what you're talking about," said Hoya. "I'm no friend of any Roller."

"I hope for your sake you're right," said Choker, circling behind and slithering up against her. "Because the next time I see him I will not be so forgiving." He smacked his baton into his hand, making Hoya jump.

"Look, Choker," snapped Hoya angrily. "I'm not interested in anything you have to say." She turned to walk away, but Choker quickly held his baton against the wall to block her path. He leaned his face in towards hers.

"Perhaps," he said, brushing his antennae over Hoya's face, "You and I might be, how shall we say, more friendly towards each other? I'm sure it would please your father to have his daughter in the care of his Lieutenant? I'm certain he would not be pleased at your affections for a Roller."

"You serve at my father's pleasure, Lieutenant," said Hoya. "I don't. And I certainly don't need *you* to take care of me. Now why don't you go and twirl your baton!"

She ducked under Choker's baton and promptly walked out of the hut, leaving the rejected Lieutenant to seethe with anger and jealousy. He couldn't understand what the General's daughter could possibly see in a Roller. But he certainly intended to teach both her and Doogie a lesson.

Outside the hut, Hoya stopped to have a moment to herself. She was shaken by Choker's threat against Doogie but also determined that he wouldn't bully her. She knew that his jealousy would boil over, and she feared that he might really hurt Doogie on the next raid. As much as she loved her father, she couldn't stand what his army did to the Rollers, nor could she let Choker get to Doogie.

Gathering her thoughts, Hoya realised that she had no choice. She had to leave the Dweller colony and find Doogie to warn him.

SEVEN

"If I don't eat some poo pretty soon, I'm going to collapse."

Clinker's portly body simply wasn't cut out for long walks through the barren African savannah. His shield, though as tough as any other dung beetle's, was used to the constant nourishment he gave it through his excessive and greedy eating. Now he was beginning to sweat and struggle, and every step felt like he was weighed down by a massive ball of dung on his back. He had fallen a little behind the lead of Doogie and Brownie, although the other ten Rollers had paced themselves behind him. The ball of dung they had been rolling along with them had supplied snacks along the way, and was now reduced to a ball that they could simply kick along in front of them.

"I must admit," said Brownie, "I'm starting to get a little tired and hungry myself." His slender frame was feeling heavy with fatigue but empty from hunger. "How far have we walked?"

"Not sure," said Doogie, who was still excited enough about the journey that he was less aware of how tired he also felt. "But it must be a fair distance. The wildebeest should be passing through here. There are grassy patches over there in the distance."

"Isn't it amazing how they turn that stuff into poo?" said Clinker, still thinking about his stomach. "Why don't we just eat the grass and cut out the middle man?"

"Because we're dung beetles, not grass beetles," answered Brownie. "And because grass tastes revolting. And it only comes in one flavour, known as…'revolting'. Whereas, depending on the beast that produces it, poo comes in lots of yummy flavours. And colours too."

"What's your favourite?" Clinker was almost salivating at the thought of his next meal.

"My favourite poo? Probably elephant. But I also like antelope poo, which is a bit of a delicacy. It's not like the mountain of stuff elephants make, but little chewy pellets. You can't roll it so you have to eat it when you find it. Something different, that's all. What's your favourite?"

"At this point," said Clinker, who was on the verge of collapsing, "I'd eat my own poo just to stay alive."

"Alright," said Doogie, who was concentrating on navigating, but acknowledged how tired everyone was. "We'll rest over there." He pointed to what looked like a large, greyish mound nearby. But as the Rollers got closer to it the haze of hot air cleared away to reveal the carcass of a dead wildebeest. It was lying on its side with its head outstretched in front of it, and there was a small pool of blood under its neck.

34

"That's weird," said Brownie. "It's mostly intact."

"What do you mean?" asked Doogie, surveying the wildebeest's large body, on which the mud was starting to dry and crack under the glaring sun.

"Well, I'm guessing it was killed by lions. You can see the bite on the neck. That's usually how lions bring down a beast. But they haven't eaten the rest of it."

"Maybe they got scared away from here," suggested Clinker.

"What could possibly scare a lion away?" Brownie mocked the suggestion.

"My farts. Your farts. Your face?" responded Clinker, mocking Brownie back.

"Guys," said Doogie. "Be serious for once."

"I'm just saying," said Clinker, defensively. "We *are* dung beetles. Makes sense to have such a defence mechanism."

"I don't think lions could give a single, solitary droplet of poo about our farts," said Doogie. "But something doesn't feel right here."

Brownie noticed Clinker walking over to the wildebeest's tail. "Where do you think you're going?"

"To see if there's anything to eat," said Clinker. The other Rollers began to follow him.

"Have a little respect, would you?" urged Brownie. "It's probably only just been killed, and you're already sniffing around its backside?"

"Hey, *I* didn't kill it," responded Clinker, shrugging his shoulders. "And I still have to eat. I'm sure this beast wouldn't mind me cleaning up its waste."

"Guys," said Doogie, turning his back to the wildebeest to face his friends. "Something's not right here. Brownie, don't the female lions bring down the beasts? And then the males come and eat first? Isn't that what happens? I'm sure that's right. I heard that somewhere, probably from you. Brownie? Brownie?"

But Brownie was frozen still. His lips were tightly pursed and he nodded rather urgently. Clinker's mouth and eyes were wide open. The other Rollers had gathered around them, all looking towards the same direction behind Doogie, who couldn't tell if they all looked petrified or constipated.

"What's wrong with all of you?" asked Doogie.

And then a thumping jet of air hit Doogie in the back, knocking him forward and almost to the ground.

"What in the name of faeces was that?!" he exclaimed, and as he turned around he saw what it was. He froze too. The jet of air had been expelled from two gaping, wet nostrils reaching over the wildebeest's body. Below the nostrils were lips that slowly peeled back to reveal a gigantic set of razor sharp, grimacing fangs. Doogie's jaw dropped down with fear as he looked further up to see the fearsome, angry eyes of the lion looking directly at him, its vast, regal mane obscuring its entire body as it stood over the dead wildebeest.

"Uh-oh."

The fangs opened apart to release a roar so deafening that it shook the entire savannah and battered the tiny dung beetles clear off their feet like a hurricane, carrying them through the air and dropping them next to a hollowed log several feet away.

"Quick!" said Doogie. "Hide inside the log!" None of the Rollers hesitated in following Doogie's advice, and scrambled over each other to get inside.

"Now would be a good time to release some of those epic farts, Clinks!" said Brownie.

A few small holes in the side of the log allowed Doogie and his friends to look outside. But something was blocking Doogie's view. Something bright yellow with a black spot in its middle was framed by a hole. Then the black spot grew in size, and Doogie realised what it was. The eye of the lion was trying to see inside the log!

"Yikes! He's outside!" whispered Doogie in terror. The eye had disappeared and was replaced by one of the lion's nostrils, which blew a gust of hot air through the hole and knocked Doogie back against the other side of the log.

"Ow! I hate it when he does that!"

The entire log began to rock from side to side, making the dung beetles fall over and onto each other. They screamed as the rocking became more and more intense, throwing Doogie and his friends against the insides of the log and sending them tumbling over each other.

The rocking stopped. "Ouch," said Clinker, landing with a thud. "That was horrible. I think I'm going to be sick."

One of the other Rollers, a young female, squeezed herself out from under the mass of bodies covering her. "Do you think he's gone?" she squeaked, in a terrified voice.

"I think maybe he's…" began Doogie, but before he could finish, a giant paw with fully extended claws reached into the log, nearly grabbing the young Roller.

"Everyone get up and get back!" screamed Doogie. "Get to the centre of the log!" Doogie grabbed the young Roller himself and flung her back behind him.

The paw continued to reach further into the log, its huge claws sinking into the wood beneath. Splinters of wood erupted and rained onto the dung beetles as the claws scratched at the floor inside. The lion growled angrily, evidently furious that the dung beetles had rudely interrupted his meal.

Doogie and the others were huddled together in the centre of the log as one giant and tense mass of dung beetles, the lion's claw reaching closer towards them. Clinker was on the edge of the huddle, trying hard to push his chubby body further into the group. Unfortunately, Brownie was next to him, and was almost suffocating under his weight.

"Clinks!" gasped Brownie. "I can't breathe!"

"Everyone just hang on!" cried Doogie. "Or none of us will be breathing ever again!"

The lion's claws scraped even further in until the tip of one claw had hooked the edge of Clinker's shield. It quickly tugged back, dragging a bewildered Clinker along the length of the scratched log floor as he screamed in fear. Before he was out of reach, Brownie quickly grabbed Clinker's leg, but the claw was too strong and dragged them both away from the huddle. Doogie grabbed Brownie's legs and the other Rollers grabbed Doogie, making a chain of outstretched dung beetles inside the log.

It worked. Clinker's slide through the log had slowed, and the claw had unhooked itself from his back. But he had reached the opening of the log, and as he rotated onto his feet he was met by the lion's enormous, snapping teeth. The terrified Clinker quickly pushed Brownie back as Doogie and the others got to their feet and ran back to the centre of the log. They stood motionless, watching as the lion's teeth continued snarling and snapping at the opening, droplets of saliva flying off and splashing inside the log. After a few huffs and puffs, the lion peered into the log with its angry eyes, glaring into its dark space and at the huddle of petrified dung beetles. And then finally the eyes pulled away and the sound of receding footsteps told Doogie and the other Rollers that the ordeal was at last over.

They finally dropped onto their backsides in relief and started to catch their breath. Brownie inspected Clinker's shield for any damage but was happy to report none. The other Rollers waited tentatively, not knowing if the lion would return. But Doogie spied through one of the log's holes and saw that the large male lion was back at the wildebeest carcass eating his lunch. Three other female lions and some cubs had joined him, all of them now with faces buried into the carcass.

"There are more of them?!" whispered Clinker, anxiously.

"Yes, but they're eating," said Doogie. "I guess he was just protecting his meal for his family. If we're going to escape, now's the time."

"Escape to where?" asked Brownie.

"There," said Doogie, pointing through the hole. And as the other Rollers followed his finger they could just make out in the distance a large herd of ambling wildebeest. "That's where the dead one must have come from. They're going to take us to Dungalore."

Doogie peered out from the other side of the log. The lions were still submerged in their meal and utterly oblivious to everything else around them. One by one, the Rollers hopped out from inside the log and gingerly tiptoed away from the direction of the lions and towards the herd of wildebeest.

EIGHT

"What do you mean 'she's gone', Lieutenant?"

General Proctor was in his hut and trying hard to contain his anger. Hoya was nowhere to be found within the Dwellers' colony and he refused to believe she had simply disappeared.

"I've checked the entire colony, General," said Lieutenant Choker, bowing before him. "She's not here."

"Well, where would she go? Why would she leave?"

"Forgive me, General, but it seems that Hoya has developed a kind of sympathy for the Rollers. I don't think she quite shares our contempt for them. I believe she has gone to find them."

"Nonsense!" barked the General in his low, gravelly voice. "She would never go to them. She knows to stay close to me."

"I'm afraid I have picked up her scent, General. And it leads in the direction of the Rollers' colony." Choker knew this information would concern his commander. And he hoped that concern would provoke the reaction he wanted.

General Proctor looked away from Choker and out through his window, into the wilderness. He remembered Hoya asking him about the raids, and her suggesting that they were cruel. Suddenly, it dawned on him that she might have had motives behind her questions. Perhaps she really had gone to find the Rollers.

Choker could see the General was thinking and seized his opportunity to make a suggestion. "General, I think we have to consider that the Rollers may *harm* Hoya, or at least take her hostage to deter us from raiding them again. I think we should be prepared to use any and all means to get her back."

The thought of anyone harming his beloved daughter made the General shake with rage. "Ready the battalion, Lieutenant," he growled. "Full complement of weapons. Find her scent. Track her down. I want her back, do you understand me?"

"Perfectly, General," said Choker, quietly smirking to himself and rubbing his hands together in self-satisfaction at his wicked ploy.

~~~

Meanwhile, Hoya had followed the aroma of spilled, raided dung all the way back to the Rollers' colony. She was giddy at the thought of meeting Doogie again and she thought hard about what she might say to him. She had made it clear during the raid that she liked him, and she knew he had always liked her.

But the colony was empty. The Rollers were nowhere to be found. Their dung huts had not been rebuilt, and scraps of dried dung lay strewn everywhere. That's odd, thought Hoya. Where did they all go? Did they simply run away? Oh no! What if they ran away? She would never see Doogie again. This was just awful!

She looked around for any sign of where they may have gone. Now that she was out here, she knew Choker would easily track her down by her scent, and his anger would then turn towards Doogie. She had to find Doogie first.

She wiggled her antennae in the air to try to capture his scent. But her attention was caught by a leaf leaning against a rock nearby. She stepped back and was astonished to find that the leaf seemed to be deliberately propped against the rock, with its pointy end facing out away from the compound. On the leaf, the shape of a triangle was smeared in dung, and inside the triangle appeared to be four letters, also faintly written in dung: DGLR.

Hoya looked hard at the leaf, wondering for a moment. And then she gasped. Followed by a smile. That crazy Doogie, she thought. He must have left that message for her! That crazy, wonderful, unbelievable dung beetle. He can't actually have gone to…? He has! He's gone to find Dungalore!

She relished the very thought of it for a brief moment. The Dwellers had heard the myth of Dungalore as well, and Hoya had heard the story when she was small. But that's all it was, wasn't it? Just a myth? He can't possibly find it? Or can he?

A sudden snap told Hoya that she was not alone. Could Choker have found her already? She held her breath and looked around her. Nothing. But something gently nudged her back. Startled, she whipped round to see an equally startled young gazelle, a male, staring back down at her with his innocent and inquisitive eyes. Hoya smiled as his head reached out to sniff her.

"Well, hello, little one," she said in a soothing voice, fully aware that she was completely dwarfed by even this young gazelle. She stretched out to his bowed head and tickled his nose, a sensation he appeared to enjoy. "Are you lost?"

The gazelle answered back by licking Hoya completely off her feet. She sat back up and laughed, and the gazelle bounced up and down and appeared to smile back at her. Then for a moment, Hoya looked down and thought.

She had an idea.

The gazelle appeared to understand that if coaxed, to let her ride on his neck, she could follow Doogie's scent and catch up with him in no time. And, perhaps Choker wouldn't be able to find them. He would be too far behind.

Hoya looked at the playful gazelle and pointed at his neck. He bowed his head down again and let her crawl up behind his ears. Higher up off the ground the air was clearer and Hoya swirled her antennae around.

And there it was; Doogie's scent.

"Okay, my young friend," she said into the gazelle's ear. "Let's go!" And she held tightly to his fur as the gazelle launched himself into the air and bounded away in impossibly long strides, quickly leaving the Rollers' colony far behind them in the distance.

NINE

The lions were now far behind the Rollers, and certainly too far away to be any kind of threat. They had managed to catch up with the marching wildebeest, being careful to stay at the herd's edge to avoid being trampled on. The herd were a constant hum of grunting and snorting, and they churned the savannah into a dense cloud of dust through which the tiny dung beetles could barely see. Fortunately, the stream of thundering hooves alongside them was more than enough of a guide.

Clinker was perfectly content. Amidst the incessant noise and choking dust the wildebeest were leaving an endless and generous stream of dung for him to munch on. It was as if he was given a new injection of energy. Doogie, Brownie and the other Rollers ate less and walked more, ignoring their instinct to roll the dung into balls.

"A beetle could set up a home amongst these guys and be happy," announced Clinker, sporting a huge, chubby grin. "I could just trail them and retire."

"When we get to Dungalore, we're going to do exactly that." declared Doogie.

"At least we won't meet any Dwellers along the way," said Brownie. "That's for sure. They are history. Old news. Not gonna hear from *them* again. Nada. Bupkiss. Zippo."

"Okay, Brown!" interrupted Doogie. "We get it."

"I'm just saying…"

"Yeah, I know. I get it." Doogie bowed his head and looked sternly at the ground, avoiding eye contact with anyone.

"What is it?" asked Brownie.

"What is what?" asked Doogie, still not looking up.

"Doogs, I know that expression on you. Something's bugging you. What's wrong?"

"Nothing," shrugged Doogie, turning his head into the wildebeest herd to hide his face from Brownie.

But Brownie persisted, this time in a more serious tone. "Doogs. What aren't you telling us?"

Doogie sighed. He knew he had nowhere else to hide or look to. And he had brought his fellow Rollers out here on this dangerous quest with him. He decided he owed it to them to tell them the truth.

"Well," he began, reluctantly turning to face Brownie. "The Dwellers might not *entirely* be history."

"What?!" exclaimed Brownie. "Why?! What did you do?"

"I may have…left something…for Hoya…to let her know…where we were headed."

48

The volcanic anger that instantly surfaced on Brownie's face erupted just as quickly. He screamed through gritted teeth while shaking his head violently from side to side in disbelief. *"You did what?! Why in the name of faecal debris would you do that?!"*

Clinker had stopped eating and he and the other Rollers had stopped moving. They stood looking at Doogie, utterly dumbfounded. The huge, lumbering legs of the wildebeest continued to plod alongside them.

Doogie had sunk his head into his shoulders, as if trying to use the shield on his back to hide. "I...didn't want her to think I just left. Without leaving a message or a note."

"So the Dwellers know where we're headed?" asked Clinker. "Oh, splat! That's just great! So much for a new life. They'll be coming for us now."

"What kind of message was it?" asked an indignant Brownie. "Did you leave them a map with directions? Did you use a *poocil* and draw them a diagram?"

"No!" said Doogie. "Of course not. I just drew a triangle on a leaf. Hoya probably didn't even see it. And even so it wouldn't matter. Choker will probably find our scent anyway."

"You think he can smell us from all the way back there?" asked Clinker.

"No, Clinks," said Brownie. "But we all have pretty sensitive antennae that can pick up any smell. And Choker's are among the best. He can pick up our scent and follow it anywhere."

Intrigued by this idea, Clinker directed his antennae upon himself. "Hey, I smell pretty good! I mean, I'm covered in wildebeest poo, but *that* smells pretty good. Hey, maybe Choker will track our scent to the lions. And then that'll be the end of him!"

Brownie shook his head and then smiled. He realised just then how strong Doogie's feeling for Hoya must be. His anger quickly fizzled out and he put his hand on Doogie's shoulder. "All right, buddy. It's okay. Let's just keep moving."

Doogie, who was still cowering with guilt, gently nodded. The Rollers continued and Clinker carried on munching his way through fallen clumps of dung. Very soon, the wildebeest brought them to the edge of a river, which, to the little dung beetles below them, seemed like a vast ocean.

The water was brown with mud and flowing fast, carrying fallen branches within its torrent. The wildebeest gathered along its edge, until the edge of the river became a wall of wildebeest, hundreds deep and stretching forever into the distance. And almost invisible at their feet was the tiny band of

Rollers perched on the muddy bank, looking confounded by the scene before them and wondering what to do next.

"Anybody want to volunteer a suggestion as to how we cross?" asked Clinker, looking anxiously at the rushing water.

Doogie stepped forward from the group, concentrating his gaze from the river back to the wildebeest, who were all tentatively dipping their front hooves into the water.

"We hitch a ride."

TEN

"You're not serious?"

As logical and rational as Brownie was, he found the idea of sailing across a massive river clinging to the back of a wildebeest to be well outside his comfort zone.

"You have a better idea? Now's the time," said Doogie.

"We'll be crushed," announced Clinker, looking worriedly from the wildebeest to the water. "And then we're going to drown. And then we're going to die."

"No one's going to drown or die," said Doogie, as both Brownie and Clinker looked at him with disbelief." This will work. It *has* to work."

"Maybe this is one of those times when we have no choice but to use our wings?" suggested Brownie.

"No," said Doogie. "Even if we flew we'd never make it to the other side. Our wings wouldn't cope. And if we fell into that water and soaked them they'd be so heavy they'd pull us under. We can't risk that."

The wildebeest were quickly resigned to somehow swimming across. One by one they hesitantly stepped forward and splashed into the water, grunting and crying in fear as they frantically paddled their hooves to stop the river's current from carrying them away.

52

"Okay," said Doogie, turning to Brownie and Clinker. "We put the group on the back of this wildebeest as it gets into the water. They can grab the mane and climb on."

"What about us?" asked Brownie.

"We'll get the next one."

Clinker slapped his hand onto his face and tugged it downwards in exasperation.

The Rollers assembled on the muddy bank and one by one climbed on top of Doogie, Clinker and Brownie to reach the long mane of a waiting wildebeest. They hurriedly pulled themselves up and onto its shoulders, just in time as it splashed forward into the water. The Rollers cried in panic as the river washed over them relentlessly, but they held on tightly.

"Just hang on!" cried Doogie. "And you'll make it to the other side!"

It was unclear if they had heard him above the deafening noise of both the grunting wildebeest and rushing water. But they held on as their ride took them slowly, but surely, across the river.

The river crashed against the dozens of screaming wildebeest that had jumped in. Twigs and branches buffeted against thrashing bodies, which had turned the water into a froth of white bubbles, as the beasts tried desperately to keep their nostrils dry. Doogie and Brownie stood and watched fixated on the soaking Rollers, not daring to let them out of their sight. Clinker found it too much to bear but was still compelled to peer through the fingers over his eyes and watch the chaos in front of him.

After what seemed like an age, the wildebeest carrying the Rollers mounted the muddy bank on the other side of the river, struggling to find its footing, before finally scrambling through the mud and onto safe ground. The Rollers carefully abseiled down its mane and dropped to the ground, barely avoiding being squashed by the fury of oncoming hooves. They turned back and made their way to the mud at the river's edge, patiently waiting to see Doogie, Brownie and Clinker on the other side.

Doogie had spotted them. "They made it!" Brownie and Clinker breathed a sigh of relief. "Now it's our turn."

The three of them waited until another wildebeest had dropped into the water next to them, and as it worked to gain its footing, Doogie, Brownie and Clinker climbed up its mane and onto its back. They were gripped with fear but focused on the mane and braced themselves for the impact of the river.

"Hold on real tight!" shouted Doogie.

The wildebeest slowly moved further into the water, resisting the onslaught of the river's current. What seemed like huge tidal waves reached over the wildebeest's neck and splashed down onto Doogie and his friends, soaking them completely. But as the water cleared out of their eyes, they were suddenly confronted with a far more terrifying sight.

The river in front of them erupted into a huge dome of frothing water, and launching up through it were the enormous, cavernous jaws of a crocodile, violently spraying water everywhere as they snapped shut around the head of their wildebeest. The force of the snap jolted the tiny dung beetles off their feet and into mid-air. As the jaws dragged the wildebeest under the surface, Doogie and his friends screamed in terror. They had landed on the crocodile's back and bounced onto its tail. Utterly petrified, they each grabbed one of the ridges on the tail and held it for dear life.

The tail was particularly sensitive and it began ferociously flailing about, trying to remove the dung beetles. All the while the enormous jaws were still pulling the wildebeest clamped inside them under the water. Doogie could just make out his friends gripping onto the tail next to him. But he couldn't speak. He was gasping for breath as the tail flew through the air and towards the water. It crashed through the surface with a thunderous crack that echoed over the river. The Rollers on the other side were witnessing the entire event, and could only look on in absolute horror. The other wildebeest were even more panicked, and furiously clambered over each other to reach the other side, their hooves scraping against anything with a surface.

Silence.

Darkness.

Doogie and his friends were underwater, still attached to the crocodile's tail. The eerie silence in the murky water contrasted with the screaming terror they were feeling and they desperately held their breath, not knowing where the tail was carrying them.

And then light appeared above them, becoming brighter and brighter. The tail sped through the water and broke the surface again, a curtain of froth in its wake.

It was too fast. Doogie and his friends had to let go of their grip and went flying once more through the air above the river. They were completely disorientated and had no sense of their bearing. They tumbled back down towards the surface, but were startled by a hard landing. Exhausted with fear, they found themselves on a large branch that had been floating by. Mercifully, it was carrying them away from the crocodile, which had by now disappeared under the surface. The branch shuddered against the side of a wildebeest and one of its twigs became caught in the beast's mane, dragging the branch along with it.

As the little beetles held onto the branch, Doogie noticed some cuts around the wildebeest's head, almost as if it had been bitten by…a crocodile! It was *their* wildebeest! It had somehow managed to get free and escape! Doogie felt a bolt of relief pierce through his fear. He couldn't believe it. He was so sure the crocodile had taken their wildebeest and drowned it.

The injured wildebeest finally found the slimy mud at the river's edge and pulled itself out of the water. Its mane yanked the branch out too, sending it splashing down into the mud nearby. Doogie checked around him to find his friends. Brownie was still on the branch, lying on his back and paralysed with fatigue.

"Brown!" cried Doogie, catching his breath. "Where's Clinks?"

"I'm here!" cried a voice buried in the mud nearby. The air was still choked with the sound of grunting and snorting, but neither Doogie nor Brownie really noticed it anymore.

Doogie looked ahead in the direction of the voice and saw a small mound of wet mud being pushed above the ground.

Then some feet emerged.

And finally, a chubby and exhausted face. "You know, if this mud was poo I could have just eaten my way out."

Both Doogie and Brownie were too tired to laugh. They lay motionless on the branch and smiled. The other Rollers had managed to find their scent and made their way through the sticky mud over to the branch.

"Are we all here?" asked Doogie, barely able to keep his eyes open.

None of the Rollers was missing.

"Okay. Good. Let's just…you know…rest …for a little bit. There's no rush."

ELEVEN

"Let's hope they don't wake up."

Following the Rollers' scent, Hoya and the gazelle had bounded their way to where the lions had feasted on their wildebeest. All that remained of their meal were a rib cage and some bones, picked clean by vultures. The lions were fast asleep, digesting and snoring. The large male was lying on his side, probably using his enormous mane as a pillow. The cubs were all resting against his belly, probably using *that* as a pillow. The three lionesses were lying on their bellies, all facing each other.

The nervous gazelle tiptoed past as quietly as he could. He knew he was food for the lions and the slightest awareness of his presence would send them chasing after him. Hoya held onto the fur behind his ears, also anxious that the lions might wake up and see them. They made it past the hollow log and continued out into the savannah.

But a sudden snap echoed out from underneath them. Oh no! The gazelle had stepped on a twig!

Hoya quickly looked behind her to see if the lions had noticed. Thankfully, they all appeared to be asleep.

But Hoya didn't notice that one of the lionesses had opened an eyelid. She didn't see the eye moving side to side, nor see its nostrils open up to inhale the air.

Feeling more confident, she looked behind her again to check on the lions.

The lionesses had gone.

The gazelle had abruptly stopped. Hoya shot her head back in front of her to find three snarling lionesses facing them, their huge, sharp teeth glistening with saliva in the sunlight. The gazelle was quivering with fear, and could barely make his legs retreat. Hoya was scared too, but summoned up all her courage to whisper into the gazelle's ear.

"Listen, we can hop out of here. One big hop and we'll be out of here."

She wasn't sure if he understood her, so she tugged hard at his ear. The gazelle sprang high up into the air. He leapt right over the bewildered lionesses, who could only watch their prey fly over them. But as the gazelle bounded away, with Hoya desperately clinging to his fur, the lionesses gave chase.

The gazelle flew with every bounce, blistering across the sprawling savannah with lightning speed and darting in every direction to shake off the lionesses. The speed lifted Hoya clear off the gazelle's neck. She struggled to hold on, eventually losing her grip from one hand. She looked down her elevated body and saw the three growling lionesses sprinting closer towards them, each from separate directions with clouds of dust trailing behind them.

Faster and faster the gazelle bounded and ran across the land, his feet barely touching the ground. Hoya couldn't see anything around her, except the blur of a landscape whizzing past. Trees merged into elephants, which merged into giraffes, which then became dust. Only the two lionesses behind her were visible as they raced after the gazelle.

Wait. Two lionesses? Where was the third?

Hoya was dizzy and faint, and barely holding on with one hand, but she looked ahead of her. There was the other lioness. Somehow it had made its way around them in an arc and now sped towards them from the front. Its savage, bloodshot eyes were bulging with fury and targeted on the gazelle with pinpoint precision. The other two lionesses behind were hounding him towards this one in front, forcing him into a trap.

But nearby, just ahead to the right, was the river. If only they could get to the river, thought Hoya, the lions couldn't follow them. She knew they hated the water. Her father had told her that once.

Her father. If he could see her now he'd be furious. What would he do? But she couldn't think about that now. There was no time. With tremendous effort, she pulled herself through the wall of rushing air and placed both hands on the gazelle's ear.

"Head for the river!" she cried. "The river! Go to the river!"

The gazelle immediately darted off to his right, forcing the oncoming lioness to lose her footing and slide across the ground as it tried to match his direction. The other two lionesses behind were still in pursuit. As the river's edge pulled nearer, Hoya and the gazelle could see it was too wide to jump. The gazelle wouldn't be able to swim. He wasn't built for swimming.

But there was a lump of rock right in the middle of the river. Perhaps the gazelle could jump onto it and then springboard himself to the other side. They were moving too fast for Hoya to instruct him in time. But the gazelle was so terrified of the chasing lionesses he didn't slow down at all. Unfortunately, neither had the lionesses. They were almost on him.

The lead lioness suddenly lunged forward with outstretched paws, her razor sharp claws fully extended. But the gazelle had jumped too, his hind legs barely escaping the claws as he soared into the air. The lioness splashed into the river below, sending a tide of water up at her two sisters just as they arrived at the riverbank.

As the gazelle descended towards the rock in the river, Hoya noticed the two yellow eyes in the water just ahead of it, ever so slightly above the surface.

It wasn't a rock. *It was a crocodile*!

It was too late. The gazelle's hooves had touched down on the crocodile's back. And just as he sprang back into the air the mighty jaws of the crocodile breached the water and twisted upwards towards him, gaping wide open underneath his legs. A horrified Hoya looked down to see the massive open jaws and rows of huge teeth soaring up towards them. The gazelle hunched his legs right up against his body, just feeling the edges of teeth scraping his hooves as the jaws snapped shut with a deafening crack. As the crocodile crashed back into the water with a thunderous splash, the gazelle and Hoya landed on the far side of the river, exhilarated with relief.

As they made it up to the top of the bank, the silhouettes of wildebeest rippled in the distant haze. And just behind them were the tiny, crawling specks of a small troop of dung beetles.

TWELVE

"I can't believe you found us!"

Doogie was overwhelmed with joy at the sight of Hoya standing before him. He never imagined that she would actually find him, or that he might see her again. She was flustered and tired but to Doogie, she looked as radiant as ever. He could not have guessed that she had just escaped the claws of lions and the jaws of a crocodile. The wildebeest had slowed down to a saunter, and the Rollers had all gathered around Hoya and Doogie.

"I got your leaf message," said Hoya, smiling at Doogie.

"Yes!" said Doogie, triumphantly. "I was hoping you would."

Clinker was staring up at the gazelle. "Who is *this* guy?" he asked.

"That's my new friend," replied Hoya. "He found me at your old compound. I think he was lost. But he's the reason I made it here. You wouldn't believe what we've just been through."

"Does he have any poo he'd like to share with us?" The gazelle playfully nudged Clinker with his nose, knocking him to the ground.

"I think he likes you!" said Hoya. Clinker grinned at the gazelle, who seemed to beam back at him. *If he likes me*, Clinker thought to himself, *he could shower me with some poo*.

"Hey, what about the other Dwellers?" asked Brownie. "Did they follow you here?"

"No," said Hoya. "But I think they will. Choker's obsessed with finding Doogie. I'm afraid of what he'll do if he finds all of you."

"We have to keep moving," said Doogie. "We can't allow them to catch up to us."

"Are you really going there?" asked Hoya. "To Dungalore? Do you really know where it is? I mean, I thought it was just a myth."

"So did we," said Brownie.

"I think I know where it is," Doogie nodded. "I think I can get us there." He looked at Hoya more intently. "What about your father? Does he know you came to find us?"

Hoya bowed her head, slightly embarrassed. "He'll probably guess that I did. He won't be happy about it. But I just couldn't stand what they were doing to you all. It just wasn't fair."

Doogie smiled and took Hoya's hand. He was so proud that she wasn't like the other Dwellers. "Don't worry," he said. "We'll take care of you. It'll be okay." Hoya looked back up at

Doogie and smiled. For a moment they stood together, reassured by each other's presence.

"Er…guys?" Clinker had stepped forward. "I hate to interrupt this beautiful romance, but does someone want to tell me who or what *that* is?"

All of the Rollers followed Clinker's anxious gaze and found themselves looking at a pale silhouette standing in front of them. It was barely visible against the harsh sun, rays of brilliant light striking out from behind it. Doogie stretched his arm out in front of Hoya to protect her, and the other Rollers edged back.

The mysterious silhouette stepped forward to reveal itself. It was a dung beetle. A strange and rugged looking one, but he had a relaxed smile and casual stance that didn't at all seem threatening.

"G'day fellas," he said, with a strange accent. "Looks like you're a little lost."

Doogie stepped forward from the rest of the Rollers. "We're Rollers. My name's Doogie." He pointed out his friends. "This is Hoya, Clinker and Brownie. And the rest of our group."

"Well, Rollers, you're in Tunnelling country now. I'm a Tunneller."

"Yeah, I've heard of you," said Brownie, drawing on his encyclopaedic knowledge. "You guys tunnel and store your dung underground, right?"

"That's right," said the stranger. "My name's Digger."

"Of course it is!" said Clinker, rolling his eyes. "What else would it be?!"

Digger smiled. "Come with me, if you like? I'll give you a tour of our colony."

"That's okay. Maybe we'll be on our way," said Doogie. He was still wary of this stranger, and certainly didn't want to reveal too much about his group or where they were headed.

"Got loads of poo if you're hungry?" said Digger.

Clinker's ears were instantly alert. "Well, I'm sure it wouldn't hurt to have a brief tour?" he said, looking innocently at Doogie. "I mean, there's no harm in looking, is there?"

Doogie smiled. "My friend here has a very curious stomach. Okay, sure, we'll take a look."

As Digger started to lead the others away, Hoya walked up to the gazelle. He lowered his head down to meet her, a pleased expression on his face.

"I think this is where we say goodbye to you, my dear friend," she said, her voice breaking. "I can't thank you enough for everything."

The gazelle tilted his head to one side and blinked. Hoya reached out to hold his nose and then gently kissed it.

"Please look after yourself," she said, tearfully. The gazelle lightly nudged her in acknowledgement and stepped back.

"Goodbye," said Hoya, and she turned and walked away with the others.

THIRTEEN

Digger led the Rollers to an opening in the ground, which became a tunnel leading under the surface. Doogie looked ahead towards the wildebeest. They had slowed down but were still moving forward.

"You're following them, right?" said Digger. "Don't worry, mate. We'll be just underneath them. You can come back to the surface further ahead, no worries."

Doogie nodded and let Digger lead him and the other Rollers down into the tunnel. It ended at an enormous underground cavern, with more tunnels heading off in all directions. The ceiling appeared to have small holes leading up to the surface, allowing beams of sunlight through to illuminate the cavern. Several dung beetles were stacking small bundles of dung against the walls, as loose soil rained down on them from above.

"Is the ground caving in?" asked Clinker.

"No, mate," said Digger. "That's just the wildebeest walking above us."

"You have a strange accent," said Brownie. "I've never heard it before."

"Well," said Digger, "We're not originally from around here. We're from some place called Australia."

"Where's that?" asked Hoya.

"Not really sure, to be honest. We came over to this land on a big floating container thing run by human beasts. Nearly starved to death too. Hardly any animals on board to supply us with food. And the humans left their waste in some kind of bowl that would make it disappear. Selfish, if you ask me. Can't see why their poo's too good for us. But we made it. And here we are. This place isn't all that different, really. Heat and sand, just like back home. The beasts here are a little different, though. But, hey, poo is poo, right?"

"You got that right," nodded Clinker, greedily eyeing the stacks of dung.

"Go ahead, mate," said Digger. "Help yourself to as much as you like. The beasts up above drop plenty for us to collect."

Without any hesitation, Clinker raced over to a stack of dung and dived straight into it.

"He likes his food, eh?" laughed Digger. "So, where are you guys heading to? You're following those beasts above, right?"

Doogie looked at Brownie and Hoya, who gave him a nod of approval.

"We're going…to Dungalore."

"*Dungalore?!*" exclaimed Digger. "I thought that was just a myth."

"I think I know where it is," said Doogie.

"It's somewhere Dwellers can't get to us," said Brownie.

"Dwellers, eh?" said Digger. "Yeah, they're a pretty nasty bunch." Doogie and Hoya looked at each other and smirked. "We don't really cross their path out here," he continued. "But I wouldn't want to run into them."

Clinker walked back over to Doogie and the others, munching away on a shiny pellet of dung. "This poo is a bit sweet," he said, studying the pellet carefully. "Where is it from?"

"I think there's something in the soil out here that makes the grass sweeter," said Digger. "So it comes out the other end a little bit sweet too. We shape it into small pellets ourselves. We call them Faeces Pieces."

"The poo in Dungalore is supposed to be sweet," said Brownie. "Maybe we're getting close?"

"Maybe you are," echoed a voice from one of the other tunnels. The voice emerged into the cavern as a curvaceous female dung beetle and walked casually towards them. She was older than Doogie and his friends, but self-confident and attractive.

"This sheila here is Dunny. She's me missus," said Digger.

Clinker stopped chewing. "Okay, you just said a whole bunch of words that don't mean anything to me."

71

"This is my wife, Dunny."

"Oh," said Clinker, cheeks full of poo. "Hi, Dunny." He carried on chewing.

"I've heard of Dungalore," said Dunny. "It may indeed be a real place. Full of sweet grass and sweeter poo."

"How come you haven't tried to go there?" asked Hoya.

"We have everything we need right here," said Dunny, looking at Digger. "Don't we?"

"Too, right, babe," said Digger. "We've had our fair share of long journeys. Our journey brought us here. And we're happy as we are."

Doogie nodded as he looked around the impressive cavern with its intricate architecture of tunnels and stacks of dung.

"You're welcome to stay here, if you'd like," said Digger. "Plenty of poo to go around."

Clinker stopped chewing again and looked at Doogie, who smiled back at him.

"No," he said. "We're Rollers. We belong on the surface, rolling our dung. It's what we know." Hoya took Doogie's hand in hers and looked at him with pride.

"Thank you, Digger," continued Doogie. "But we have to get going."

"No worries, mate. I understand. We'll show you the way out."

Doogie, Hoya and the others squinted as the scorching sunlight outside once again hit their eyes. The wildebeest were still just ahead of them, ambling along, grunting and snorting.

But as the dung beetles reached the surface, a low gravelly voice bellowed out from behind them.

"Well, well, well. If it isn't my daughter and her merry band of Rollers."

FOURTEEN

"Dad?! How did you find us here?"

Hoya, Doogie and the others were more surprised than scared. Assembled before them was a sprawling battalion of Dwellers, all armed with sharpened twigs, with General Proctor and Lieutenant Choker in the chariot at their centre.

"We're Dwellers," growled General Proctor. "There really isn't much we can't do. I would think my only daughter would know that better than anyone."

Hoya was blushing with shame. Part of her was reassured to see her father again, whom she cared for deeply, but she also knew he was very disappointed in her. She hadn't yet worked out how to explain herself to him.

The General continued. "I raced here thinking my daughter was in danger, that she needed my help. Choker was tracking your scent all over the savannah. But here you are running with the Rollers. I cannot believe my daughter would betray me."

"I'm not in danger, Dad," said Hoya. "And I never set out to betray you. But I stand with my friends. I can't allow you to hurt them anymore. It's just wrong."

Lieutenant Choker suddenly lunged forward, pushing his muscular frame through the assembled Dwellers and stopping just in front of them. His face was scrunched into a look of fuming anger.

"What's wrong," he shouted, "is that you would abandon your own kind to be with these weaklings. Have you no loyalty?"

"She's a dung beetle," said Doogie, stepping between Hoya and Choker. "She's the same kind as all of us. She's just not a bullying thug like you!"

"Silence, Roller!" shouted Choker, crazed with fury, as he raised his baton to strike Doogie. "We're going to eliminate every last one of you!"

"No!" cried Hoya, and she pushed Doogie out of Choker's way, taking the painful blow from the baton herself.

"Hoya!" cried an anguished General Proctor, shocked at the strike on his daughter. Choker was stunned and immediately stepped back, unsure of what to say.

Hoya, fallen on the ground and crying in pain, looked up at Choker. "And where will you take your dung from after you get rid of all the Rollers?"

It was all too much for Doogie. Completely overwhelmed with rage, he got to his feet and lunged for Choker, grabbing his baton and trying to shake it free from his hands. But Choker simply lifted his baton into the air, Doogie along with it, and punched Doogie back into his friends, knocking Clinker and Brownie both over as they tried to catch him.

The General watched on from his chariot. He wasn't one to show emotion, but he was starting to feel uncomfortable. Choker's uncontrolled anger concerned him, and it had already caused injury to his daughter.

"Choker," he said. "Step back."

"But General," implored Choker. "We have them where we want them. Now is the time to attack. We can get rid of them all!"

And before waiting for the General's response, Choker signalled to the Dwellers. "Bring out the Defecator."

From behind the lines of Dwellers appeared a bizarre looking contraption. Four wheels of rolled dung supported a hardened dung platform between them. And mounted on top of it was an enormous oval cannon facing up at an angle. The back of the cannon appeared to be tethered to the end of the platform.

Doogie was on his feet and holding Hoya. The other Rollers stood behind him, looking nervously at the contraption.

"Load it up!" shouted Choker, at which several Dwellers rolled out small balls of dung and placed one of them inside the cannon. The General looked on, becoming more uncomfortable with each passing moment.

"This is what we call poetic justice," said Choker, a malevolent grin creeping onto his face. "These are balls of dung we stole from you."

Doogie turned to the General. "General. Why would you allow this? We're all dung beetles. We should be working together, not fighting each other. We have too much in common. There's nothing to be gained from all this hatred and anger. If we work together, just imagine what we could do, how much dung we could harvest. That's why Hoya is here. She knows this. And I think you must too."

The General took a moment to think about Doogie's words. He had been a soldier all his life, and expected the same of his daughter. And yet here she was, asking him to abandon his ways and change what he thought he was. He was torn inside. Choker was doing his bidding, but Hoya was his only daughter.

But Choker would not allow any delay. He pointed to the Defecator.

"Fire!"

The cannon roared as the ball of dung shot out and into the air.

The Rollers looked up as the ball descended towards them, its growing shadow casting darkness over them before landing on Clinker and knocking him to the ground.

"Clinks!" cried Brownie. "Are you all right?"

"I think so," said Clinker, emerging from a heap of dung. "It actually tastes pretty good."

Doogie smiled smugly at Choker, who only became more furious.

"Load it up again!" shouted Choker, and the Dwellers heaved another dung ball into the front of the cannon.

"General!" cried Doogie.

"Dad!" cried Hoya. "You can't let this happen!"

The General looked at Choker, who was about to order another firing of the Defecator.

But everyone was interrupted by a low rumbling underneath them. The ground gently shook and both the General and Choker looked around them, startled and confused. It felt as if the ground was about to fall in on itself.

Mounds of dirt erupted everywhere around the dung beetles. Many of the Dwellers were tipped to one side as mounds erupted under their feet. They were appearing all around them, popping up in quick succession and turning the flat savannah into a carpet of muddy bumps.

A rather large mound appeared next to Doogie and Hoya's feet, clumps of soil pouring out onto the ground.

And emerging through the mound was a familiar face.

FIFTEEN

"G'day folks! Looks like you're in a spot of bother?"

"Digger!" cried Doogie, overcome with relief at the sight of a friendly face.

Hundreds of Tunnellers began to emerge from the mounds until they were surrounding the Dwellers. Choker didn't know which way to look, for in every direction he was faced with a Tunneller.

"What is this?" shouted General Proctor from his chariot. "Who are all these beetles?"

"These are our friends, General," said Doogie, confidently. "These are Tunnellers."

"They are of no consequence," said Choker. "If they decide to stand with you, then they will share your fate." He turned once again to the Defecator, which was loaded and ready to fire.

"Dad!" cried Hoya, stepping forward to reach her father. "You need to stop this! Look around you. We're all dung beetles. We all just want to live and eat our poo in peace. No one needs to be harmed. No one has to suffer. You can stop this. You can!"

The General, welling with sympathy as he looked at his daughter, started to slowly nod his head. But it was too late.

"Fire!" screamed Choker.

General Proctor looked on with alarm as the dung ball soared through the air and raced downwards towards the Rollers.

Digger quickly ushered the Rollers out of the way, placing himself in the path of the dung ball. Just as it was about to land on top of him, he quickly jumped out of the way and let the ball fall and disappear through the hole in the ground from which he had emerged.

Choker was not amused. "You just wasted a perfectly good dung ball," he sneered.

"That's not a dung ball," mocked Digger. His fellow Tunnellers rolled forward a huge ball of dung from behind him, as tall as Choker himself. "*That's* a dung ball."

He grabbed Choker, spun him around and shoved him right into the dung ball, which collapsed all over him. "There you are," said Digger. "Choke on *that*."

Doogie and Hoya were amazed, having to hold their hands up to their mouths to contain their laughter. Clinker and Brownie were clapping and the other Rollers were cheering. The Dwellers were shocked, never having seen anyone subdue their lieutenant.

The General stepped down from his chariot and walked up to the Rollers. "Enough!" he boomed. "Choker! Get up right now!"

Choker emerged from the collapsed dung ball, fists clenched and bursting with anger. Digger looked at him and smiled, completely relaxed. Doogie and Hoya looked on in anticipation, wondering what would happen next.

But no one had anticipated what happened next.

For the briefest moment everyone saw the silent, fluttering shadow speeding through them along the ground. Doogie barely had time to focus on it before Hoya was suddenly wrenched away, caught in the vice of gigantic talons. As she was lifted up her feet connected with Choker, knocking him back into the collapsed ball of dung. Everyone's shocked gaze turned upwards.

General Proctor reached out to the sky in desperation. "Hoya! No!"

But she was soon out of range. All the dung beetles were silent and could only look on in complete horror as the eagle flew up into the sky carrying Hoya with it. But it didn't disappear. Instead, it glided over the herd of wildebeest and back towards the dung beetles.

Doogie saw something strange on its legs. What appeared to be pink blotches above its talons. It looked like it had been burned. He kept his eyes fixed on the eagle as it landed in a distant tree in the middle of a small copse.

Doogie's horror immediately turned into recognition.

"I know that eagle! I know that place!" he said aloud.

"My daughter!" cried General Proctor. "She's gone!" His grief turned to anger, directed at Doogie. "You made this happen! She should never have come here!" And the General clasped his hand around one of the batons on his belt.

"General!" shouted Doogie. "Wait! I know how we can get her back. That very same eagle took me a few days ago. And I escaped. I know how we can save her!"

"What are you talking about?" asked the sceptical General. "How could you possibly have escaped an eagle?"

The Dwellers and Rollers all gathered around the General and Doogie. Digger and the Tunnellers listened in too.

"General," said Doogie, "You have to trust me. I want Hoya back as much as you do. But we have to work together if we're going to get her back. We have to put away our differences and you have to put down your weapons. We have to work together as dung beetles. It's the only chance she has."

General Proctor looked at Doogie and then at all the other dung beetles around him. They all seemed to implore him to listen to Doogie. He considered Doogie's words carefully and finally decided that his daughter's safety was far more important than subduing a few Rollers.

"All right," he said. "We'll do it. What do you have in mind?"

The tense Rollers, including Clinker and Brownie, breathed an audible sigh of relief.

But Choker had just gotten to his feet. "You're not seriously considering this, General?" he asked. "We came here to defeat the Rollers, not help them."

"We came here for my daughter," said General Proctor. "And now she's gone. And I will do anything necessary to get her back. I order you to help us."

"Help these weaklings?!" cried Choker. "Never! They're the reason she's gone!"

"Either you help us, Lieutenant," said the General. "Or you leave us."

Choker was embarrassed, his pride immeasurably hurt. His hatred of the Rollers was still raw and deep. His authority had been undermined and the Rollers were the cause. He looked around at all the faces watching him. Then, he ran across the savannah until he disappeared into the haze of hot air.

General Proctor bowed his head in dismay. Then turning to Doogie he quietly asked, "What do you want us to do?"

"We need to get past the wildebeest and over to that tree where the eagle landed," said Doogie. "I think it must have a nest up there. If we can get to it, we can have a chance of saving Hoya before…" Doogie paused for a moment. He really didn't want to think about what might happen to Hoya if they didn't rescue her.

"Let's just get there as fast as we can," he said, and then looked past the Dwellers at the Defecator.

"And bring that thing with you."

SIXTEEN

"Are you sure that's what you want us to do?"

Digger was no stranger to crazy ideas, having used plenty of them to journey from far away Australia to here in Africa. But this idea from Doogie seemed to be the most outlandish he had ever heard.

"I'm sure," said Doogie. "I know it sounds crazy, but it has to work. I know you guys can do it."

"No worries, mate," said Digger. "Leave it to us. We'll get it done."

Digger and his groups of Tunnellers quickly burrowed back into the earth below and disappeared.

"Where are they going?" asked General Proctor.

"General, we don't have a lot of time," said Doogie. "We have to get to that tree in the distance. That's where the eagle took Hoya. We have to get up there."

"And how do you propose we get up there?" asked the General. "It's too high up for us to fly. Our wings aren't cut out for that height."

Doogie looked over at the Defecator. "That's how."

The General didn't quite understand, but time was ebbing away. He knew they had to get going before anything else happened to Hoya. With Doogie riding with him in his chariot and the Rollers and Dwellers alongside, they raced across the dusty savannah, weaving through the legs of wildebeest and ducking under their hooves and heads.

But they were not the only ones headed for the tree. A lone giraffe had spotted some tasty twigs on the branches and cantered its way over. As the dung beetles approached, the giraffe's legs towered over them, reaching high up to a slender body with a beautiful patchwork pattern. And extending from this body was an incredibly long neck that stretched up to the branches in the trees. It was so high up it barely noticed the army of dung beetles gathered around its feet.

"Wow," said Clinker, nearly falling on his back as he looked up to see the giraffe. "That's a really big cow."

"A giraffe," said Brownie. "The tallest animal on Earth."

"Let's hope it produces the tallest pile of poo on Earth," said Clinker.

"Okay," said Doogie. "Here's what we do. General? Can we modify the Defecator to launch a beetle instead of a dung ball?"

General Proctor looked at Doogie quizzically. "I suppose so. We need to make the hole bigger at the front. We can cut the launch bowl in half. That will open it up."

And then the General paused. "Why?"

Doogie smiled and looked up at the giraffe's enormous neck. Suddenly Doogie's plan was starting to make sense.

The Dwellers wasted no time. They surrounded the Defecator, completely smothering it. When they had cleared away from it, the oval launcher was now half its length. The skinny end with the small hole had gone, leaving a giant bowl facing upwards.

"We'll use it to get us up onto the giraffe's neck," Doogie explained, "and from there we can climb up into the tree. The nest is in one of those big branches."

"Then that's where Hoya is," said General Proctor. "I can detect her scent. She's there. Probably scared out of her mind."

"We'll stay down here," said Brownie. "In case…you know…something happens…down here."

"Yeah," said Clinker. "Like if the giraffe does a poo."

Doogie shook his head and rolled his eyes before joining the General in the modified bowl of the Defecator. A small group of Dwellers had gathered to its rear, ready to launch them.

"Okay," said Doogie, turning to his friends. "When you get the signal, run away from this tree as fast as you can. Just go."

"What's the signal?" asked Brownie.

"You'll know it when it happens," replied Doogie.

Doogie and the General looked at each other anxiously.

"Let's do this," said Doogie.

"Fire!' bellowed the General.

The Defecator shuddered to life and shot Doogie and the General up into the air and onto the shoulder of the giraffe. They grabbed its fur with all their feet and struggled up towards its head, which was busy munching away at the leaves. From far down below, the other dung beetles looked on with baited breath, as two small black spots slowly inched up the giraffe's neck.

But the giraffe suddenly felt the strange sensation. Its long, narrow head lowered down and twisted towards Doogie and the General. It sniffed at them, before a long, black tongue pierced through its lips and licked at its neck beside them. The tongue, perfectly elongated to strip branches of their twigs, and as long as the neck was wide, instantly gave Doogie an idea.

"General!" cried Doogie. "When the tongue comes back this way, we grab it!"

Sure enough, the giraffe sniffed them again and the snake-like tongue reached out towards Doogie and the General. They pushed themselves off the giraffe's neck and grabbed hold. General Proctor only managed to grab the tongue with two hands, his feet dangling underneath as the giraffe swung its head back up. Flying up towards the treetop, Doogie saw the ground below them become even more distant and his fellow dung beetles moving like black dots. Both Doogie and the General were terrified of falling such a long way down.

The giraffe's head reached the treetop and rested onto a branch. Its retracting tongue forced the General to let go and he landed on the branch with a gentle bump. A moment later, Doogie landed on top of him. But they had made it. It felt like being at the top of the world, and the curious giraffe sniffed at them again before walking away.

"There goes our ride down," said the General.

"Don't worry," said Doogie. "If all goes to plan, we won't need it."

Their attention turned to the eagle's nest, which was cradled by a few branches on the other end of the tree. The eagle was nowhere to be seen. Doogie and the General hurried along the branch they had landed on, pushing leaves out of their way and hopping over small twigs.

"Wait," said Doogie. "We need some of these leaves."

"Why?" asked the General.

"Just trust me," said Doogie. "Grab some of them."

The General and Doogie collected some of the citrus leaves, tearing them away from their stalks, and carried on towards the nest. But the General noticed that the leaves were starting to make his hands itch, and soon the itch became a burning sensation.

"Doogie," he said. "These leaves. They're starting to burn."

"I know, General," said Doogie. "Just hang on."

Finally, they reached the eagle's nest, and peered over its edge. To their delight and relief, Hoya was there and still alive. But she was clinging to the sides of the nest and desperate to climb out. She was terrified. And just below her was the reason why.

SEVENTEEN

"Dad! Doogie! Help me!"

"Hang on, Hoya! We'll get you out of there!"

Doogie hadn't anticipated that the nest would be occupied. But as Hoya held on desperately to the far side of the nest, two eagle chicks below her were squealing relentlessly, their beaks jutting into the air and opening for anything that might drop in. Their young, hairless bodies seemed utterly helpless, a complete contrast to their fearsome mother.

Doogie and General Proctor raced around the edge of the nest to where Hoya was holding on. They put their citrus leaves down and reached into the nest. Hoya grabbed both Doogie and the General's arms, pushing upwards with her feet. But as they lifted her out, a familiar shadow blanketed the nest. The branches shuddered as they looked up into the darkness.

The mother eagle had landed. And she was furious.

Her fury was mixed with surprise at seeing unexpected visitors at her nest. Her eyes glared at the dung beetles and her massive wings were raised and unfolded. She quickly arched her head across the nest, covering her chicks with her neck, and grabbed Hoya's legs in her beak. Doogie and the General were still holding her hands and pulled her towards them in panic. Hoya's body was stretched out over the nest, the little

91

mouths of the eagle chicks snapping at her just below. They were expecting her to fall in at any moment.

"Help! Help me!" screamed Hoya, numb with fear.

"She'll be torn apart!" cried the General.

"The leaves!" cried Doogie. "The leaves! Roll them up! Hurry!"

Realising there was no time for questions, the General let go of Hoya and rolled up the leaves. Doogie held tightly to Hoya's hands, but they were slipping out of his. The eagle was just too strong. He was losing her.

"Throw them!" cried Doogie. "Into its mouth!"

The General threw the roll as hard as he could into the eagle's beak.

The burning sensation began instantly and the eagle screamed with pain, letting go of Hoya's legs. Doogie and the General grabbed at her arms and pulled her out of the nest. The chicks snapped at her, just scraping under her soles with the tips of their beaks. The eagle flapped her wings violently, sending twigs and leaves raining down to the ground. The very leaves that she had hoped would deter any predators from stealing her chicks were now burning her own mouth. She flew up onto a branch above, screeching in pain.

Hoya immediately threw her arms around Doogie and held him so tightly with joy that he could hardly breathe. The

General looked at them both, and in that moment he realised how much his daughter cared for Doogie. He was surprised to find himself filled with pride. Hoya let Doogie take a breath and she threw herself at her father, who held her just as tightly.

"I thought I wouldn't see you again, Dad," she said.

"Impossible," said General Proctor. "I'd never let anything happen to my little girl." As she hugged him again, he saw Doogie smiling at them and added, "But we would never have reached you if it wasn't for your friend here. I suppose I was wrong about him. Perhaps about many things."

Hoya kissed her father on his cheek. She was so relieved to hear him say that.

"Okay," said Hoya. "Now what? How do we get out of here?"

Doogie looked down at the ground. "It should be happening by now," he said.

"What should be happening?" asked General Proctor.

And soon the rumble began. Quietly at first, it quickly roared up from the ground and shook the entire tree. Doogie, Hoya and the General were knocked off their feet but landed on the branch under the nest. The tree kept shaking and swaying from side to side, the branches rattling and cracking. The roaring and rumbling became even louder, almost drowning out the eagle's screeching. As Doogie looked down, he saw the ground erupting all around the base of the tree. Earth spewed up and flew everywhere, a fog of dust clouding the view as the tree slowly began to sink. The ground was swallowing it up.

"Alright," said Doogie. "Get ready to jump."

"Jump?!" cried Hoya. "But we're so high up!"

"We won't be for long."

The eagle, still in pain, grabbed the nest in her burning beak and flew up high into the sky. Doogie, Hoya and the General watched below as the ground came closer towards them. The air had become saturated with dust and flying earth, and within seconds the treetop was just above the ground.

"Okay," said Doogie. "Jump!"

All three of them jumped off the branch onto the erupting mound of earth just below them. They rolled down the rubble until they met the flat ground of the savannah. As they looked back, just a few twigs at the tip of the treetop were visible before disappearing below the mound. The tree was gone.

"How did that happen?" asked Hoya, catching her breath.

Her answer poked through the mounds of dirt and earth and appeared as dozens of Tunnellers. Digger broke through the mound too, emerging in front of Doogie.

"Guess your plan worked, then, eh?" said Digger.

"You planned this?" said Hoya, looking at Doogie in amazement.

"Well, I…er…yeah," said Doogie. "I guess I did."

"Incredible," said General Proctor, holding his hand out to shake Doogie's. "I don't suppose you'd consider leading a battalion? You'd make a good soldier."

"I'm not interested in fighting, General," said Doogie. "I don't think we need to fight. I mean, do we, really?"

The General hesitated. "It's…it's always been our nature."

"It's not in any of our natures to climb up giraffes and fight eagles either," said Doogie. "Maybe we've proved that we can be better than nature intended."

The General bowed his head and gently nodded, before looking at Doogie again. "Thank you, Doogie. You saved my daughter. You saved us all."

"Yeah, good job, Doogs," said a familiar voice. And through the dust appeared Clinker, then Brownie and the other Rollers. The Dwellers appeared behind them, all slightly bewildered.

"That was some signal," said Brownie. "Well done to you too, Digger. You guys are amazing."

"Cheers, mate," said Digger. "We like to think we can make the Earth move under your feet."

"Wait, where did a giraffe come into it?" Hoya asked her father.

"I'll tell you about it another time," said General Proctor.

Dusk had soon descended upon them and the sun had given way to the Moon and stars. The dust settled quickly and the endless savannah once again stretched out before them. But something was different about it. The wildebeest had gone. There was hardly a beast around. Just an eerie emptiness surrounded them.

But Doogie was motionless, his eyes wide and his mouth open in disbelief. Everyone followed his fixated stare over the hole in the ground and towards the distance. Then they saw it too.

And they simply couldn't believe their eyes.

EIGHTEEN

"Is that what I think it is?"

Hoya held Doogie's hand, expecting him to answer. But he was speechless at what he saw. The other dung beetles had gathered around him, transfixed on the scene in front of them.

"How is this possible?" asked General Proctor. "It's not supposed to be real."

"Seems real enough to me, mate," said Digger. "Looks like you guys made it."

"You mean…we're here?" said Brownie. "We found it?"

Everyone slowly walked past where the tree had stood moments earlier and looked up at the darkening dusk sky. The Constellation Big Dumper was sparkling brightly above the long valley in front of them. Beasts of every kind and from every place were gathered together there, feeding on a carpet of shimmering green grass. Glints of moonlight shone from tiny leaves on small trees dotted throughout the valley, and a flowing stream of bright teal water wound its way through the centre of the valley towards the mighty pyramid at its end.

Elephants brushed up against wildebeest, which brushed up against zebras. Antelopes and gazelle found space amongst them, sharing in the bountiful grass. Several giraffes strode through the herds, picking at the small leaves on the trees. And all along the sides of the valley, huge piles of fresh, steaming dung were neatly standing like sentries guarding the valley. It was almost as though the beasts wanted to keep the valley unspoiled, leaving all their dung at the sides.

"Look at all that poo!" called Clinker, almost breathless with amazement.

"That's how they keep the grass so green, I suppose," said Brownie. "Plenty of dung to fertilise it."

"We should get down there." Doogie turned to the General. "I guess you'll lead your beetles down there with us?"

"Yes. Yes I will," said the General. "I can't believe this place is real. The pyramid...the valley...it really exists?"

"Yes," said Doogie, a huge smile forming across his face. "This is Dungalore. And we're going to live here."

Doogie turned to Digger. "How about you? Are you coming with us?"

"Dunno, mate," said Digger. "Looks too nice a place to be digging up."

"Well, just see what you think. You can always turn back if you don't like it."

"Fair enough." Digger signalled to the Tunnellers to follow the other dung beetles.

Down in the valley the dung beetles pushed their way through delicate blades of grass, looking up at the huge beasts standing above them. The elephants' trunks swung alongside them, and the wildebeests' hooves stepped out of their way. It was as if they were welcome here.

Clinker grabbed at morsels of dung lying at the feet of the beasts. "It's so sweet," he said.

"The grass is sweeter here," said Digger. "My dear Dunny was right. I should have brought her with me."

They reached the stream and gathered at the water's edge. The colour of the water was unlike anything they had seen before. Under the brightening Moon, the water appeared bluer and glowed and sparkled like a precious stone. A large water lily had become detached from its stalk under the water and floated along the surface to where the dung beetles had gathered.

Doogie turned to Brownie, hoping to harvest his vast knowledge.

"Brown," said Doogie, "Can we use this water lily to float to the pyramid? Will it hold our weight? Is it strong enough?"

"Sure," said Brownie. "It should comfortably hold all of us. Why do you want to go there?"

"I don't know," said Doogie. "I feel like it's where we're supposed to go."

All the dung beetles climbed onto the water lily and pushed themselves away from the water's edge. General Proctor instructed the Dwellers to use their batons to row at the sides. Doogie and Hoya stood together at the front of the water lily, as the pyramid grew closer and larger.

"What do you think is inside there?" asked Hoya.

"I don't know," said Doogie. "Brownie said humans built it a long time ago. I don't think there's anything inside it now."

"It's a pile of rocks," said Clinker. "Who cares what's inside? We have all the poo we could ever want out here."

"I know," said Doogie. "You're right, Clinks. But it might be worth a look."

Both the Moon in the sky and its reflection in the water were like twin beams, lighting the way to the pyramid. The dung beetles sailed past the beasts quietly munching on the grass at the stream's edge. There were no predators in the valleys, such as lions or hyenas, and no crocodiles in the water. Everything seemed very peaceful and all the beasts were completely content.

They had finally reached the foot of the pyramid. It was absolutely enormous and seemed to tower over them and reach far up into the sky. Its top nestled neatly between the points of light that made up the Constellation Big Dumper. Countless layers of huge stones reached up to the top, all perfectly sealed together. The stream flowed into the base of the pyramid through a small opening just ahead of them. And above the opening, carved into the stone, was the shape of a dung beetle.

General Proctor ordered his Dwellers to stop paddling, but they already had. They were mesmerised by the pyramid. The water lily just sat on the still Moonlit water, with the dung beetles standing on it and looking up.

Digger walked over to Doogie. "Can you feel that, mate?" he said.

"Feel what?" said Doogie.

"There's something moving in the water. Something underneath us."

"I don't feel anything."

Doogie looked at the water around him. There wasn't even so much as a ripple in the stream. But Digger was visibly concerned.

"Tunnellers have sensitive feet," said Digger. "We can sense vibrations from miles away. I really think there's something underneath…"

Before Digger could finish his sentence, bubbles started to appear in the water in front of them. A few bubbles became many, and they became larger and larger. The water lily began to rock from side to side, until all the dung beetles tried to regain their balance.

Through the bubbles in front of them an island appeared to emerge slowly from the water. It had a domed surface, shiny grey and glistening under the Moonlight.

"This could be bad…" said Doogie.

As the island kept rising, another smaller island emerged in front of it, but this one had an eye at each side. And appearing in front of them were two huge nostrils, and then a wide mouth. It stopped moving, and simply stared at the dung beetles before it.

"Well, that doesn't seem so bad," said Clinker.

"It's a hippopotamus," announced Brownie. "They spend most of their time in the water."

"I bet it has fantastic poo," said Clinker.

"If it lets us get past alive, you can ask it," said Doogie.

"I doubt it'll hurt us," added Brownie. "After all…"

But Brownie stopped as the enormous mouth began to open. Wider and wider, revealing a massive pink tongue inside a deep black hole. The front of the mouth was guarded at each corner by gigantic pillars of teeth, the biggest the dung beetles had ever seen.

From the deep darkness of its mouth a shadowy outline emerged, walking onto the tongue.

As the shadow walked forward, the Moon touched it with a finger of light, illuminating a terrifyingly familiar frame that Doogie and Hoya recognised only too well. And then it spoke.

"Miss me, everyone?"

NINETEEN

"Choker?!"

Everyone was in shock. The air was silent and the water lily was motionless. The hippopotamus held its mouth open. And standing proudly on its tongue with his hands on his waist was Lieutenant Choker.

"I…I don't understand," said Doogie. "How did you get here?"

"Lieutenant," said General Proctor, stepping forward. "What is the meaning of this? Why are you here?"

"Hows and whys are not important, General," said Choker. "I'm here now. And I do not intend to share this place with these vermin." On his last word he pointed at Doogie.

Doogie clenched his jaw in anger at Choker's insult. He took a position in front of Hoya, who stood in front of the General.

Digger casually walked to the edge of the water lily and looked Choker in the eye. "Listen, mate. This isn't your place to share. It doesn't belong to anyone. It's a big enough place for all of us. And if it wasn't for my Roller friend here, you wouldn't even have thought to come here."

Choker showed his teeth in a furious grimace, then jumped off the hippo's tongue and onto the water lily. The shudder from his landing caused many of the dung beetles to nearly lose their footing. Choker slapped Digger so hard that he sent him flying into the water. He then grabbed Doogie by the neck and held him aloft.

The hippopotamus closed its mouth behind him and began to sink back down below the surface. Only a few remaining bubbles provided any evidence that it had been there.

"You are the worst of them all!" screamed Choker at Doogie, who was struggling to breathe with his tightening grip. "I'm going to finish you off for good this time!"

"Put him down, Choker!" said General Proctor. "That's an order."

"I don't take orders from you anymore, General," said Choker. "I'll be giving them from now on."

"No!" screamed Hoya, and she threw as many kicks and punches at Choker as she could muster. But Choker laughed at her and slapped her off her feet. General Proctor turned crimson with rage and ran at Choker. He flew into him with such force that Choker, Doogie and he all went tumbling into the water with a tremendous splash.

Hoya got to her feet, watching the three bodies disappear under the water's surface. She knelt down by the edge of the water lily, waiting with anxious anticipation. The other dung beetles had gathered behind her.

The passing moments felt like an unbearably long time.

"Should we go in after them?" asked Clinker, anxious for Doogie's safety.

"I don't know," said Brownie. "I don't think we can swim. How would we get out?"

Hoya barely heard them. She was looking ever more intently into the water, tears strolling down her cheeks. The Moonlight offered nothing but a reflection of herself.

Then, suddenly, the water erupted in front of her. Water sprayed everywhere as two hands landed on the edge of the water lily. It was Digger.

"Digger!" cried Hoya, immediately helping him up onto the water lily. "My Dad? Doogie? Did you see them?"

"I don't know," said Digger, trying to catch his breath. "I didn't see anything. I barely made it back to the surface. I'm definitely not made for water, that's for sure."

The water erupted again, drenching both Hoya and Digger. It was General Proctor. Hoya rushed to help him. She hugged him tightly, glad as she was to see him.

"Dad? What about Doogie? Is he okay?"

"I...I'm not sure," said the General. "It's so dark under there. I couldn't see anything."

Hoya knelt yet again at the water lily's edge. General Proctor and Digger stood behind her, soaking wet. The other dung beetles crowded in even closer.

"Come on, Doogie, come on..." whispered Hoya to herself, hoping beyond hope. She gritted her teeth and scrunched the water lily's edge in her fists, overcome with anxiety. It seemed like an age had passed, each moment more and more desperate. Doogie had been down there so long, it was uncertain if he could still be alive.

But the water splashed hard against Hoya's face, and through the falling droplets she saw Doogie in the water coughing and spluttering and gasping for air. She reached out to him, grabbing his hands, and pulled him to the edge of the water lily.

"Thank goodness!" cried Hoya. "I was so scared! But you made it!"

Doogie was fighting so hard to get his breath back that he couldn't speak.

"What happened to Choker?" asked Clinker.

Everyone looked down at Doogie, waiting for his answer. Breathing hard, he looked back up at them and simply shook his head.

"He's gone?" asked General Proctor.

"He won't be bothering us again," said Doogie, climbing back onto the water lily. "Ever again."

Hoya grabbed Doogie and hugged him hard. General Proctor put his arms around them both.

But everyone's relief was short-lived. The water lily jolted and began to rise. The dung beetles had to quickly regain their footing. The entire water lily began to rise up out of the water. A familiar grey and shiny island emerged around them.

"Is it Choker?" asked Hoya.

"No," said Doogie. "This is something else."

"It's the hippopotamus," said Brownie. "We're on its back."

Indeed they were, and the hippopotamus's eyes emerged ahead of them, this time facing the pyramid. It began to slowly move forward, inching towards the opening under the carving of the dung beetle. The water lily rested neatly over its rounded back as it sailed forward into the darkness, carrying its dung beetle passengers with it.

"It's taking us into the pyramid," said Clinker.

"Yep," said Brownie. "It sure looks that way."

"I'm scared," said Hoya. "It's so dark in there."

"Don't be scared, my dear," said General Proctor. "We've come this far and survived. I doubt anything could stop us now."

"What do you think is inside there?" asked Digger.

"I don't know," said Doogie. "But we're going find out. Let the adventure begin!"

Other 2013-14 GB Publications

Mary Pargeter

isbn
9780957297043

journey in shades (Pub: 2013)
poetry in light and dark

Professor Carol Rumens, Guardian Books Online 'Poem of the Week' blog: "I have felt engaged with the work, and responsive to its emotional charge."

Jay Ramsay, Caduceus Journal: "She lets detail speak, often exquisitely, through things as they are; there is no attempt to escape through fantasy."

Female First online magazine, Lucy Walton interview with Mary Pargeter.

Cpt George P Boughton

isbn
9780957672826

Seafaring – The Full Story
(Pub: 1926, Epilogue added 2013, Prologue added 2014)

Times Literary Supplement: "His book is genuine sea salt...warm colours of Mr Shoesmith's pictures accord well with the romantic story" of days before steamships

John O'London Weekly: "An excellent book"

Lloyds List & Shipping Gazette: "one of the best books on life at sea that have been published for many a day"

The Spectator: "recalls emotions [on sea-life] that have fleeted from the minds of most"

The Traveller's Gazette, Thomas Cook: "All will read the pages of 'Seafaring' with unalloyed pleasure"

Blue Peter Journal, AT Stewart Commander Royal Navy: "This book is stamped with the personality of a thorough seaman, the sea-breezes [and chanties] stir in its pages"